REVIEWING THE MURDER

DOG DETECTIVES - THE BEAGLE MYSTERIES

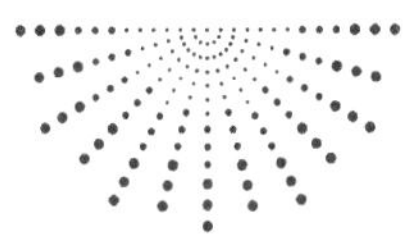

ROSIE SAMS

AGATHA PARKER

SWEETBOOKHUB.COM

THE DOG DETECTIVES – THE BEAGLE
MYSTERIES

Welcome to my new book. I joined forces with the amazing Rosie Sams to work on this wonderful series of cozy mystery books all featuring a sweet little Beagle puppy. Mazie is an ex-police dog who was wounded in service. She is gifted to Hannah Barry, a broken-hearted realtor who is down on her luck.

At first, Hannah is unsure, can she learn to love the Beagle? What will she do when a body is found?

If you missed it, find out how Mazie found a new home, and Hannah some peace, in this fabulous box set of the first 6 books.

Dog Detective – The Beagle Mysteries Book 1 to 6

Rosie has a free book Smudge and the Stolen Puppies that you can pick up. It is about an amazing and cute French Bulldog the best Dog Detective in all of Port Warren. Grab it here for FREE

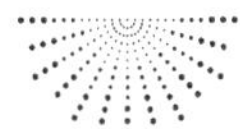

Colin rushed around his kitchen in Troughton's Trough shuffling sizzling pans across the gas stove top. He was the owner and chef of an upscale restaurant in the small town of Blairstown, Vermont, and he had a big night coming up the next day. Nerves didn't normally bother him but the pressure was intense and he wanted everything to be great. Opening the oven to remove the rack of lamb, he grabbed the pan with his bare hands. "Ouch!" he yelped, snapping his hand back.

"Everything okay in there?" Hannah peeked in the kitchen when she heard her boyfriend's cry of pain.

"Everything is fine. I'm just a little nervous about tonight. Well, actually, tomorrow night, but this night reflects directly on that one," he said, sweat beading on his forehead.

Hannah noted his nervous chatter and moved into the kitchen to wrap her arms around his waist. "It's going to be amazing. You are born to do this."

He gave her a nervous grimace.

"I'll be out there to support you. You've got this," she whispered. She threw out as many words of affirmation as she could think of, hoping he had been convinced. She, of course, believed everything she said, as did the rest of the town. His restaurant was a local favorite. But she knew he was struggling with self-doubt right now and she wanted to be sure he felt her encouragement down deep in his bones. She kissed him quickly on the cheek before slipping back out of the kitchen.

Colin was hosting a small tasting party that evening with his closest friends in attendance. Hannah was right. He was a great chef, and he loved everyone who was coming. He had gathered his nearest and dearest for a special tasting menu in preparation for a visit from Wyatt Flynn. A famed food critic with an acid-laced pen. Wyatt's review, if positive, could make Troughton's Trough a hot spot for tourists passing through the area for years to come. Or it could do exactly the opposite.

The food critic was due to eat at the restaurant the next evening, and Colin was testing his recipes on his best friends this evening.

Colin took a deep breath and pushed the kitchen door open with his back, soup in hand. He plastered on a big smile in order to build his own confidence and the confidence of his patrons. Placing the soup in front of each of his friends with a flourish, he said, "Bon Appetit!" Glancing around the room, he hoped his forced enthusiasm was believable. He wasn't used to feeling these nerves, especially in the company of his closest friends.

Kate Carver, the local police chief was there with her boyfriend, Niles. Niles was also Hannah's cousin. After taking a single bite of the split pea soup, each of them raved about its flavor, even asking for seconds.

When Colin came back with the rack of lamb, oven mitts *on* this time, his close friends, Oscar and Anita, complimented him profusely. They'd never tasted lamb so tender or full of flavor. Oscar and Anita Gomez owned a local coffee shop, Jolt of Java, where he and Hannah often frequented.

When he brought out the dessert of cherries jubilee, the last of his dishes, Colin finally allowed himself to sit at the table to join his guests. He looked to Hannah who smiled back at him, but he suddenly realized, he hadn't heard a word from her throughout the whole tasting. Had there been something wrong with his food? She would tell him, of course, wouldn't she?

He watched as she tossed her tricolored beagle, Mazie, bits of bread between each of her own bites of food. He observed as she took a small bite of her dessert, chewed it, and then swallowed. Still, she said nothing.

"What do you think, Hannah?" he asked, nerves bubbling he was unable to wait a moment longer.

She looked up to match his gaze with hers, but she was expressionless. Then she lifted her hand next to her face, crooked her index finger, and gestured for him to join her in the kitchen. Colin discreetly excused himself, nerves shooting through him as he imagined what she might say. Had something been wrong with his food, and she was trying to tell him in private to save him the embarrassment?

He rushed to follow her into the kitchen. When they were alone, he spoke quickly. "I know, I was so doubtful about his meal. I should have gone with something classic like chicken, but I was feeling overconfident in my rack of lamb. I know everyone was just being nice out there because they are my friends but thank you for being willing to tell me the truth. Lay it on me, Hannah. I can take it. Say whatever you need to say. It's better for me to hear it today than tomorrow... after Wyatt Flynn has tried it!"

He ran a hand over his chin stubble. "And thank you for bringing me in here to save me the humiliation from the others. You'll prepare me for what Wyatt will inevitably say. Please, lay it all on the line." He finally stopped talking and took a deep breath.

Hannah took a step towards Colin and cupped his face between her hands. "Colin, listen to me."

Colin closed his mouth and waited for her to break his heart.

"Everything this evening was phenomenal. I mean that. The food was flawless," she said. "I only brought you in here to tell you in person how exquisite the meal was, and also to show you my appreciation in private." Then she got on her tiptoes and gave him a tender kiss.

Colin relaxed in her embrace and wrapped his arms around her letting out a big sigh. "Oh! What a relief!" He dipped his head to rest on her shoulder for a moment. Then he looked into her eyes. "Your approval is more than enough. Thank you, Hannah. I can't tell you what this means to me. As long as I know you love my food, I'll be okay," he said.

"Well, I'm happy to hear that," Hannah said smiling. "But I still want Wyatt Flynn to give you a rousing endorsement, and I think you are well on your way to achieving as much. Tomorrow night is going to be a smashing success." She reached up to give him one last kiss on the cheek, before leading him back out to his guests.

CHAPTER TWO

*H*annah woke the next day to a beautiful stream of sun coming through her window. Mazie jumped on the bed and began licking her face. "Okay, okay," Hannah laughed. "Let's go for a walk." Mazie knew the meaning of that word and hopped off the bed, scampering to her leash hanging at the front door.

After securing Mazie's harness, the two of them walked outside and moved along their familiar path around the block. Mazie knew the way, sniffing her favorite flowers on her favorite lawns the whole time, as Hannah appreciated the fresh blooms coming in. She'd been a realtor in her previous career, and still appreciated the details of a home. She noted that a neighbor had painted their shutters, and another one had put out new flowers on their porch. She waved at some children playing soccer in their front yard and overall enjoyed the ritual.

As they rounded their second corner, Hannah was surprised to see Liesel Richter running in her direction. The woman looked somewhat frantic, her hair on end, her eyes wide. "Liesel! How are you doing this morning?" Hannah asked.

Liesel marched towards Hannah as if on a mission. Hannah noticed the sun glint off of something shining in her hand. She was carrying a – knife?

"Hannah," she said, slightly breathless.

"How are things at *Gutes Essen* going these days?" Hannah asked with a forced cheer, wondering why Liesel was holding a knife. She guessed that it had something to do with her own kitchen; Liesel owned another of Blairstown's dining establishments, but hers specialized in German cuisine.

"That's exactly what I want to talk to you about. I saw you and Mazie walking, and I rushed out of the kitchen to chase you down," she said, concern furrowed between her brows.

A flood of worry shot through Hannah. What exactly could this be about? It sounded serious.

"I've heard that Wyatt Flynn is in town." She lowered her voice. "That man is a foul individual, you need to be on the lookout. Please, warn Colin as much." She fiddled with the knife in her hand, absentmindedly twisting its handle in a circular motion.

Hannah was taken aback by her statement, but also how cryptic she was sounding. "What exactly do you mean?"

"I mean, he destroys lives with his caustic reviews," she explained. Her eyes darkened as she referenced the man.

"But why should we be worried about the man? I've seen him in pictures, and he seems a little gruff, maybe, but otherwise harmless." Hannah thought to a recent magazine article she'd read and pictured the profile picture of the short mustachioed man with shaggy dark hair and matching dark eyes.

"He does come across seemingly harmless. In person, he's almost forgettable. Certainly not friendly, but not physically dangerous in any way. That's not what I mean. I'm talking about when he puts pen to paper," she said.

"Is this coming from personal experience?" Hannah asked.

She nodded solemnly and lowered her voice. "He came to *Gutes Essen* once. I thought everything went well at the tasting, I even managed to pry a smile from the man. He gave no indication that anything was wrong. Looking back, I realize he gave no reason that anything was right, either, but then his review was published." Her eyes narrowed and flitted to the side as if she were picturing his words on the page. "Needless to say, his review was a negative one. I mean it was acid-laced. He talked about the dust on the floorboards of the restaurant, which by the way, had been cleaned the day before! When he talked about the food it was obvious that everything was cooked to perfection, but not to his preference. I do understand that taste is subjective, but as a professional food critic, you are supposed to suspend your own tastes somewhat, and approach things in a neutral way." She watched Hannah's reaction carefully, then continued "And listen, I understand that in this industry you need to have a tough skin. And I do! But his review was so scathing, and in my opinion, unfair, that I remember every word of it."

Hannah felt sad for the woman. "Oh, Liesel, I'm so sorry. That must have been hard."

"What was hard, is that people *still* reference it. All this time later! It's as if I can't shake what he said about us. Just remember, Hannah. The internet lives forever. Colin may get a positive review, but will it be worth the risk if he doesn't?"

Hannah's ears perked at this. She hadn't considered that a potential negative review could cling to Colin's reputation for years to come.

"Potential customers will call the restaurant and consider a reservation, but they will want to go through Wyatt Flynn's review word for word, just to ask questions and seek clarification. Then ultimately most of them opt to take their business elsewhere!"

Poor Liesel looked exasperated. Hannah couldn't help but feel sorry for the woman, while also inexplicably wanting to put distance between them. "I'm so sorry to hear that, Liesel. And thank you for the heads up. I will tell Colin what you told me, but I'm afraid I might be too late. Wyatt is already scheduled to come to Troughton's Trough tonight. I'm afraid it's all up to chance now."

"It's never too late to cancel," Liesel corrected her. "There, I've said what I had to. I couldn't live with myself if I didn't warn you."

Mazie had been pulling on her leash during their conversation, and finally managed to put her front paws on Liesel's leg, her snout in the air, trying to sniff the knife.

"Careful!" Hannah called to her dog, afraid she would get hurt by the sharp blade.

Then, as if Liesel finally noticed that she was carrying a knife, she looked down at it. "Oh! I'm so sorry. I was slicing bratwurst and ran right out here when I saw you go by the window." She lifted the knife away from Mazie. "All right, I'll get back now, but I feel better having said something to you," she said.

I'm glad someone feels better, Hannah thought as she bid her goodbye. All of Liesel's worry seemed to have transferred directly to her. She and Mazie continued on their walk, Hannah hoping that Colin would fare far better where it came to Mr. Flynn's pen.

Instead of walking back home, Hannah took a slight detour to her own office. She was a private investigator and had a storefront right next to Troughton's Trough. The bells rang when she unlocked the front door. She tossed Mazie a treat on her dog bed and sat herself down in front of her computer. She wanted to do a little bit of snooping. Or rather, research about the things Liesel had just told her.

She typed the name of the local German restaurant into the search bar and waited to see what would come up. Sure enough, Wyatt Flynn's negative review populated near the top of the search. She clicked on it and went to the comments section. There were a mix of responses, some agreeing with him, some refuting him but as Liesel had said, the damage had obviously been done.

Then she began looking through some of his other reviews and found out that the fate of the German restaurant was hardly unique. For every favorable review, Flynn wrote about five others that were overly critical. The more Hannah read, the more she became worried that Colin could fall victim to the same fate. Her mind started to spin as she began fearing for what a negative review could do to Colin's bottom line in the long run.

CHAPTER THREE

That evening, Hannah showed up to Troughton's Trough dressed in an elegant black dress. Understated but stylish, she was ready for the big event. She went to meet Colin in the back room of the restaurant, where he had texted her to find him.

She opened the door to see her good-looking boyfriend, usually cool under pressure, sweating profusely and looking anything but. Beads formed on his forehead as he tucked his starched white shirt into his black suit pants. He looked up to see her and tossed his hands up as if to show her something. "I'm shaking too badly to even get dressed!" he said.

Hannah moved toward him and straightened his tie. She folded his collar over it and held his suit jacket up for him to slide his arms into. She picked up a napkin from the side table and gently dabbed his forehead with it. "Colin," she whispered, "you've got this." She said it in a way that she hoped instilled confidence in him, but something about her demeanor must have caused him to pause.

"Hannah, you seem tense, is something going on?"

She was taken aback by his keen observational skills, even in his moment of stress. A testament to how close the two of them had become – he knew her very well. She had gone back and forth in her mind all day about whether or not to say anything about her conversation with Liesel. She didn't want to be the reason he canceled on Wyatt Flynn, knowing that the press that would come from that could be as bad as a negative review. Combined with that fact, she truly felt Colin's food was top notch. She looked at him now, and seeing how nervous he was she still couldn't decide what to do.

"No! Not at all," she said, averting her gaze from his.

Then Colin shifted gears and began to comfort her. "Please, don't be nervous for me. I'm more than ready to face Wyatt Flynn tonight. I've been slaving over a hot stove all day. Everything is looking and smelling delicious. These are dishes that I'm fully confident in.

Everything is going to be great," he assured her. "Last night's trial run went off without a hitch, I have the same confidence in this evening."

Hannah felt bad that her boyfriend was trying to comfort her in his big moment. She debated about whether or not to tell him what she'd found online that day, but what good would it do to mention something now? On the other hand, could she forgive herself if it all went badly, and she had a chance to tell Colin beforehand? After all, it wasn't technically too late to pull the plug on the evening. She decided to go for it.

"Okay, I found something," she said.

Colin froze. "What is it?"

"I ran into Liesel Richter today," she began, still deciding how much to say. "She told me that Wyatt came to review her restaurant once. He left such a scathing review that her business is still suffering. She seemed intent on telling me this and wanted me to pass the message along."

Colin shrugged. "Okay. Now you did your duty. As much as I do feel bad for Liesel, that's just the industry. Maybe she had a bad night in the kitchen."

"That's just it Colin," Hannah said, deciding now to tell him everything. "I did some research today, I spent a long time looking into this guy, actually. His reviews seem to be arbitrary at best. It seems like what he writes is directly dependent on whatever his mood is that day, rather than the quality of the food. I'm just worried that if he's had a bad day, he's going to take it out on your food. What if your best isn't good enough, and it puts Troughton's Trough at risk?" she asked.

Colin's face fell. He scanned her face as he thought through what she'd just told him. Finally, he put a hand on her shoulders and spoke. "I am confident that I will be the one to buck the trend. I'm not only great in the kitchen but I'm also good with people. I am sure I'll be able to win Mr. Flynn over, bad day or not."

Colin seemed to have recovered from the bomb she dropped, but Hannah couldn't help but question whether he was putting on a brave face, or if he meant it.

"Mark my words, Hannah. Troughton's Trough will be one of the few who manages to win Wyatt Flynn's seal of approval," he said with his chin in the air.

Hannah silently hoped that his confidence would cause his sentiment to be true. "I hope you are right," she said. "And it's important to remember that no matter how this evening goes, you have already won my vote, in every way, shape, and form." Hannah tilted her chin up to give him a kiss and Mazie yipped her approval from their feet.

Colin pulled away, laughing. "That was just the good luck charm I needed!" he said.

Mazie moved to her bed to settle in for a nap. She would wait in the back room during dinner, so the food critic wasn't distracted by her. Colin even had his sous-chef prepare a special dinner for the beagle as he felt bad leaving her out of the party.

"Ready?" Hannah asked.

"As I'll ever be," Colin answered.

Hannah took his arm and they walked to the dining room, prepared to greet Wyatt Flynn at the start of the night's service.

No sooner had the two of them entered the dining room than the front door opened to reveal a short, dark-haired man with a prominent mustache, twirled up at the ends. "That is definitely him," Hannah whispered, recognizing him as if she knew him from all of her research that afternoon. She gave Colin's hand a quick squeeze as a silent "good luck," and let him go to greet the food critic.

She watched as Colin's tall frame confidently covered the distance between her and the critic. Colin extended his hand to the shorter man. "Welcome to Troughton's Trough!" he said enthusiastically.

The man looked up at Colin, expressionless, and shook his hand. Hannah watched Wyatt's knuckles turn white as he squeezed Colin's extended hand. "You will need to do much to impress me this evening, young man," he said.

Hannah thought that the age difference between them couldn't have been more than ten years. And even still, Colin was a fully formed adult. It seemed like a strange power move to reference him in that way. She unconsciously gritted her teeth as she watched the stout man move across the dining room and sit at his appointed table.

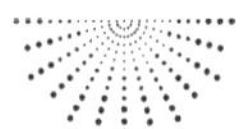

CHAPTER FOUR

Colin had only his best waitstaff on hand that evening to help serve Mr. Flynn; he wasn't about to take any chances with the event. He wanted the critic's experience to be top-notch, from walking into the restaurant to the service, and of course, the food itself.

He didn't know this, but Hannah had sneaked into the restaurant that day to dust the baseboards, just in case; there was no detail left to chance.

It didn't take very long for Colin to feel grateful about his decision to take such careful precautions. His staff served Flynn each course of his meal, with Colin himself stopping by to check in on him after every dish. The gruff man insisted on using his personal metal straw to sip each beverage, but he also insisted that the beverage be changed for every course. He wanted a comprehensive wine pairing for the meal. This meant that between each course, a server had to thoroughly rinse the metal straw, so he could taste the wine in its pure form.

Colin refrained from mentioning that a metal straw diluted the purity of the wine's taste, choosing to honor the critic's odd request instead.

Hannah watched as Colin stood obscured behind a corner wall in the kitchen holding his breath when he wasn't out chatting to the critic. He would peek at the food critic as often as he dared without being seen by the man. Hannah could see that he was starting to worry. Wyatt hadn't so much as said a word with each course that had been brought out to him. It was anyone's guess as to how much, if at all, he was enjoying the meal. Again, this tracked with what Liesel had told Hannah but did nothing to calm her own nerves. They wouldn't know what the man thought until his review was published.

Hannah was beginning to wonder if he'd done enough to receive a favorable review. Despite pulling out all the stops, the words of Liesel rang in her ears. Was it all arbitrary? Before she could think about it too much longer, the sound of chair legs scraping violently against the hardwood rang in her ears. She turned to see a woman with royal blue hair stand up. Hannah recognized her as a patron who had been eating quietly in the corner, but now she was anything but. She snapped her fingers to call attention to herself, which was unnecessary, as the whole room was already looking at her.

"Hello, everyone!" she announced at a decibel just a step below yelling. "My name is Clair Darrow."

Hannah noticed Flynn visibly flinch when the woman said her name. She couldn't help but note that it was his first sign of emotion the whole evening. Then, to Hannah's astonishment, Wyatt scraped his own chair back and stood to face Clair from the opposite side of the room. His face was near purple as he clenched his fists open and closed at his sides. "Before that horrid woman continues to speak, allow me to assure you all that there is no sense listening to a second-rate food critic! It's all theatrics. Her vlog, her taste, her opinion!" he shouted.

Each jaw in the restaurant collectively dropped. Heads swiveled to Clair to hear her retort.

The blue-haired woman scoffed and continued. "Ha! Big words from such a little man indeed! Mr. Flynn here has been running scared since my video blogs have been gaining more attention, more traction, and more views than poor Wyatt's old-school newspaper articles ever will." Clair lifted her chin in the air as if to say, 'checkmate'.

"Not true!" Wyatt yelled back.

Clair snapped her fingers once more, this time at her assistant, Jordan Redding. A man with deep brown skin came running to her side, tablet in hand. He brought the screen to life and handed it to Clair. Clair strode across the floor of the dining room towards Mr. Flynn and shoved the tablet in his face. Jordan followed close behind her.

Wyatt turned his head to the side as if the tablet was an afront to him. "Allow me," Jordan said, pressing play on the video he had queued up. A professional quality video began to play, highlighting the exterior of Troughton's Trough, then cutting to the interior, panning over the elegantly decorated tables, and finally, zooming into the sizzling rack of lamb that had just been delivered to the table. Clair's voiceover could be heard over the images, discussing the meal she'd just eaten in detail. She was gushing about every aspect of her experience.

Clair crossed her arms over her chest as she scanned the crowd. It was as if she was on stage and was trying to avoid her back being turned to anyone. "As you can see, *my* vlog is already live. Anything you try to write will no doubt not only land with a thud but also be completely irrelevant after people see this video. No one is looking at your old school articles anymore, my friend." At this, she placed a hand on Wyatt's back, causing him to jerk himself away. "I'm afraid it's time to face the facts."

Wyatt's face changed to a darker shade of purple. A vein in his forehead was now swollen and throbbing. He clenched his fists again but now seemed unable to find words to defend himself. Instead, he turned and stalked out of the establishment.

The diners watched him leave. It was only when the door closed behind them that they started back up with their conversations, whispering to one another about the scene they had just witnessed. Clair took the opportunity to approach Colin. "Mr. Troughton, thank you for the opportunity to dine at your fine eatery this evening. I enjoyed every inch of my meal here. You have an exquisite touch in the kitchen." She offered her hand for Colin to shake.

He reached to grab it. "Why, thank you, Ms. Darrow. My only regret is not knowing you were coming this evening."

"Oh, please call me Clair!" she said. "And nonsense. I like the element of surprise. We appreciate eating meals that are prepared when the chef does not know we are coming." She gave him a little wink and gestured to Jordan that it was time to leave. "We'll be seeing more of one another, I'm sure of it." Then she turned on a single heel and she and Jordan left the restaurant.

Colin stood stunned in the center of the restaurant, taking in all that had just transpired. Hannah moved over to him, looping her arm through his, and guided him to the back room. He wordlessly sank into a chair. He ran his fingers through his hair and looked to Hannah. "Was all the planning for Flynn's arrival less than necessary?"

"It's never a bad thing to prepare," Hannah replied. "I'm sure Clair's experience here was just a little bit more crisp than usual, which must have helped some, to be sure. That said, it does seem as though our worries about what Flynn would say are no longer an issue."

Colin nodded, obviously relieved. "No kidding. What a weight lifted that is. I was putting on a good face when you told me the news about Liesel, but I have to admit I was pretty nervous," he confessed.

There was a loud knock at the door and Hannah moved

to answer it. Standing there were their good friends, Anita and Oscar. "May we come in?" Anita asked.

Hannah widened the door. Oscar took a seat next to Colin. "Check this out," he said showing Colin his phone. "We have both been receiving several notifications since Clair posted her vlog." Hannah moved behind Colin to look over his shoulder at Oscar's phone and saw almost a dozen new notifications. All about Troughton's Trough.

"How did you get all of these?" Colin asked.

"We subscribe to all the local culinary alerts, just to keep abreast of the food scene in Blairstown. Our food selection is minimal, but we like to know what's trending," Oscar explained.

Hannah rubbed Colin's shoulders reassuringly. "It's been a successful night, one way or another," she said. Colin murmured his agreement. Though that was true, Hannah had been watching Wyatt Flynn carefully throughout the evening, and she had noticed his anger. She couldn't help but feel concerned about what he might try to do with it all. The rage in his eyes was roaring, and she wondered if he might somehow turn his anger on Clair.

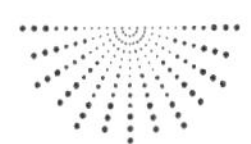

CHAPTER FIVE

When service for the restaurant had finally finished for the evening, Colin began cleaning with the rest of his crew. It was something he normally saved for his employees, but something about the events of the evening had him feeling the need to scrub pots therapeutically. With Colin's back hunched over the industrial sink, scrubbing away, Hannah announced that she would be right back, she was just going to take Mazie for a quick walk.

He turned to her. "Okay, be safe, take your phone."

"Will do," Hannah said as she moved into the dining room. Spotting Kate and Niles drinking an after-dinner espresso, she went to their table. "Either one of you care to join me on a little evening stroll?"

Niles jumped up. "I'd love to. I could use the chance to stretch my legs. Kate?" he asked his girlfriend.

"Sounds lovely," she agreed, standing to join her friends. The three of them, plus Mazie, made their way into the crisp evening air. "Where to?"

"I was thinking we could pay a visit to the Wentworth Inn," Hannah replied.

"Oh? Any particular reason?" Kate asked her eyebrow rising quizzically.

Hannah smiled mischievously. "As it happens, I think a certain Mr. Flynn is staying there."

Niles chuckled and walked on. "The Wentworth Inn it is, then."

After a short walk, the three of them arrived at the Wentworth. Hannah had been in the little hotel a few times, each time she had been able to convince the front desk clerk to give her the information she needed. She hoped this time would be no different. She asked Niles and Kate to stay near the entrance while she approached the desk.

"Hi, there!" she said cheerily. "How are you tonight?"

The clerk looked up from his worn paperback and eyed her over the rim of his bifocals. "Oh. It's you."

Hannah stifled a laugh. "It is me, again. I was just wondering if – "

He held out his hand. "Save me the theatrics. What's the name?"

Hannah reached into her back pocket to withdrawal a gift card she'd snuck from Troughton's Trough. She'd found out that this clerk loved lamb, and she knew that Colin prepared the best lamb in town. She'd done this once before and was pleased to discover that it worked again. "Wyatt Flynn," she replied.

He took the gift card and typed something into his computer. "224," he said without looking up.

"Thanks," Hannah whispered, then made her way back to Niles and Kate.

Kate stood waiting with her head cocked. "Everything that just happened was legal, I hope?" As the local police chief, currently dating another officer, Hannah knew she wanted things to be clean. It was also why Hannah had them wait away from the desk. She ignored the question, instead gesturing for them to follow her. Plausible denia-bility, she figured.

They rode the elevator to the second floor, then followed the numerical signs to room 224. Hannah knocked and stepped back to wait with the others. Within moments, the door swung open. Standing on the other side of it was a curvy brunette. "Yes?" she said in a velvety smooth voice.

Hannah jerked back in surprise. Maybe her deal with the clerk downstairs wasn't quite as foolproof as she had thought. "Oh, I'm so sorry. I thought this was Wyatt Flynn's room."

The woman smiled. "It is! I'm his assistant. It's nice to meet you, my name is Nina Trent." She extended her hand to Hannah. "And who are you?"

"I'm Hannah Barry," she replied. "I'm dating Colin Troughton, who is the wonder of Troughton's Trough."

Nina nodded her head in recognition of the restaurant's name.

"Wyatt left the restaurant abruptly, and we just wanted to come to check on him to be sure he was okay."

"Come in, then," Nina said, opening the door for them. They all followed Nina into the hotel room and took a seat in the sitting area at the foot of the bed. Nina poured herself a glass of rose and asked if anyone else wanted one. They all shook their heads no.

Settling back into her chair, tucking her feet beneath her, Nina wasted no time for small talk. "Wyatt was an absolute mess tonight. He called me and launched into an absolute tirade about Clair's vlog. He insisted that I find one of his industry contacts and find a way to take the silly thing down." Nina smirked and sipped her drink.

"How did you respond?" Hannah asked.

"Oh, I listened, and agreed, I assured him I would do my best, I told him all he needed to hear. But honestly, it was never going to happen. I just needed to give him some time to calm down."

"Has he calmed down yet?"

"That, I don't know. I haven't spoken with him since. There is no talking to Mr. Flynn when he is feeling cornered; believe me, I've learned *that* from experience. He needs his space." Nina shrugged and took another sip of her wine. "What can I say? He'll come around; he always does."

Hannah reached over to place her hand on Nina's arm. "Thanks, Nina. We will be in touch if you don't mind. We want to be sure he's okay."

"Yes, of course. I'll be sure to keep you posted," she said. Hannah noticed that she flinched slightly and moved her arm away from Hannah's grasp and fiddled with her hair. It was then that Hannah noticed Nina's sleeve fall down to her elbow revealing a fresh bruise around her wrist. She tried not to focus on it, in case Nina noticed her doing so. Instead, she redirected her line of questioning.

"Is there anything else you'd like to tell us about Mr. Flynn's behavior?" Hannah asked.

Nina's eyes flashed to her bruised wrist and quickly brought her other hand over to cover it. "Nothing," she said quickly. "I am fully capable of taking care of myself." Standing abruptly, she moved to the door. "It's time for everyone to leave," she said faking a yawn. "I'm feeling so tired suddenly."

Hannah knew she'd found as much out as she was going to, and reluctantly followed Nina's instructions, Kate and Niles followed her lead. Meanwhile, Mazie took the opportunity to dart under the bed in the hotel room. "Mazie!" Hannah called after her dog. "Leave it, it's time to go!" She looked at Nina apologetically. "Maybe there's food under there, I'm so sorry. She's very smell-oriented."

Hannah lowered to her hands and knees, trying to lure Mazie out from under the bed. Finally, the beagle scooted her way out, only to emerge with something between her teeth.

"Is that what I think it is?" Kate asked.

Hannah, who was eye level with her tricolored beagle confirmed. "It is. It's Wyatt's straw!"

They all stood around the beagle, looking down at the same silver, reusable straw they all recognized from its frequent use that very evening. The question on everyone's mind was, *where was Wyatt?*

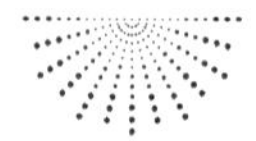

CHAPTER SIX

*N*ina placed her wine glass down and jumped to her feet. "That, I can explain!" she said.

Kate, who'd so far been silent as Hannah worked her Private Investigator magic, slipped into "cop mode" and began interrogating Nina.

"You said Wyatt had not come back to this room. The straw indicates that is obviously false," she said. "Why did you lie?" Kate left the question hanging in the air. Hannah knew from experience that Kate would be willing to sit in indefinite silence while she waited for Nina's response. She focused her gaze on Nina. "Are you hiding something?"

Nina stood squirming, darting her gaze from the floor to the television, avoiding any eye contact at all costs. "No, I'm not telling the truth, I mean lying. I mean... I'm not hiding anything!" she said, exasperated. "I just mean that I can explain.

"Nina," Hannah finally said in a soft voice. "Nina, your bruises."

Nina instinctively covered her wrist, while Kate's tone turned sympathetic. "I think it's obvious to everyone in this room, and outside of this room, for that matter, that Wyatt Flynn is a jerk," Kate said. "We want to help you. It's not going to do you any good to protect him, Nina."

Nina nodded, seeming to relax just slightly. "I agree, Wyatt is difficult. There is no arguing that."

Kate seemed to seize the opportunity and added, "I could understand, of course, if things got out of hand with a man like that." Hannah watched Nina carefully to see how she'd respond, if she would soften in any way.

Instead, her eyes fluttered up and she glared at Kate as if she just caught her meaning. She furiously shook her head. "It's not what you think. There is no way I would murder Wyatt, or even harm him at all. I truly respect him and his work. He's a culinary genius, you know. It's not often you come across someone with a palate as discerning as his. You really should cut him a break. He has or had so much going on in his brain at one time, it was just too much to expect that he also be friendly to people. That's not his job! It's not his fault that his office is in public. He was there to judge the food, not make friends!" she babbled on and on as if trying to convince herself.

Hannah couldn't help but think that Nina sounded like someone in an abusive relationship who'd been conditioned to not only say those things but to believe them as well.

Hannah and Kate stayed silent, waiting for her to continue.

"I mean, fine. Flynn might have come back to the room after the restaurant. Yes, okay? I admit it, he was here. And okay, maybe he'd been a little rough with me. You have to understand that he didn't mean it, he was just frustrated, and angry, and humiliated." She looked between Kate and Hannah. "As you would be if that young punk of a vlogger came into your place of work and ridiculed you publicly! But there's nothing more to the story. I suggested we get out of town. Leave this place and ignore what happened with Clair. This angered him, and he grabbed me by my wrist, I wriggled away. The bruise is a misunderstanding. If only I'd been still, it wouldn't have bruised at all. Really, it looks much worse than it is. I'm sure he'll turn up in short order."

Hannah was saddened to hear the way Nina spoke about herself and Wyatt. Their relationship was obviously dysfunctional, and at the very least, Hannah wanted to help free her from Wyatt's psychological grip on her. She opened her mouth to say as much but was interrupted by the shrill ringing of Kate's cell phone. They all watched her look at the caller I.D. and purse her lips.

"This is Kate Carver," she answered.

After listening and murmuring in response, she hung up the phone. Turning to the group, she said, "I have some bad news. A body has been found." Then she directed her focus to Nina. "I'm so sorry, Nina, but it's Wyatt. It's your boss's body that was found."

Nina's eyes filled her face and a scream was ripped from her. Stuffing her hands in her face she stifled it and slumped down into her chair. With a face as white as chalk, she started to tremble.

Hannah grabbed a blanket from the bed and wrapped it around Nina's shoulders.

Wanting to give her some space, she moved to Kate to confer about the finer details of the call. It had been Ralph on the phone. He was calling to let Kate know that an elderly couple had been going for a nice evening stroll along the same block that Hannah and Mazie often took and came across a pair of feet sticking out from behind some cinderblocks in an alley. The man evidently loved to collect treasures from other people's garbage and thought that the shoes he saw were about his size. To the nice couple's horror, the shoes were attached to a pair of feet, which were attached to a body. A dead body. They called the police right away, and Ralph was first on the scene. He was able to identify the body as Wyatt Flynn's and called Kate immediately.

After their hushed whispers back and forth, Kate stepped away from Hannah. She moved to Nina and placed a comforting hand on her shoulder. "I really am sorry about the timing of this, but unfortunately, I have no choice in the matter. I have to take you in for questioning."

Hannah had no argument against the logic. She felt bad for Nina, of course, but she knew it was the right move to make. In her heart, she didn't think Nina was the killer, but there was a chance she was keeping some information from them. Hannah moved back to Nina. "I'm so sorry, Nina, but Kate is going to have to take you to the station for questioning."

The woman looked up, shocked. "No! For what? I'm completely innocent in all of this – you were all literally standing with me in my room while he was murdered. You are my alibi, what could you possibly want from me?"

"Technically, we don't know when Wyatt was murdered. Which means it may have happened before we got here. Which means you theoretically had the opportunity."

This caused Nina to begin shrieking. "It wasn't me!"

Kate nodded to Niles for assistance in escorting Nina to the station. She didn't have her patrol car, but she called Ralph, her assistant deputy to come to the Wentworth Inn.

"It's just protocol, Nina," Kate assured her. "Come on with us."

Nina wiped a tear away from her cheek and reluctantly allowed Niles to escort her to the lobby.

Hannah watched the pitiful scene of Nina, wrapped in the hotel's blanket shuffle across the lobby to the waiting police car, her face streaked with smudged mascara, and couldn't help but feel a sense of doubt. Nina may be a suspect, but Hannah was doubtful that it would come to more than that.

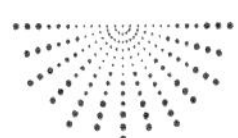

The next morning, Hannah sat with Colin and Anita at Jolt of Java - Oscar and Anita's cozy coffee shop. She fiddled with her coffee cup, hardly sipping it at all. She watched as Colin was glued to his phone, since the vlog from Clair had gone live, he couldn't look away from his phone, tracking the comments and views of the flattering video. Reservations at Troughton's Trough were booked through the end of the month, something his upscale eatery had never before experienced. Hannah stared at him waiting for him to finally look up.

When he did, he said, "Clair Darrow's review has been so incredible for business. I can hardly believe my luck."

He looked back down to continue scrolling through his phone.

Hannah couldn't help but think the unexpected attention he was receiving was starting to go to his head. She cringed at the thought of this going on indefinitely.

"A well-deserved congratulations to you, Colin!" Anita said. "You have worked so hard at your restaurant; I can't think of someone who deserves it more."

"Thank you, Anita. That's really kind," Colin said, genuinely appreciative of Anita's praise.

"You know, on top of the customers you are getting from Clair's vlog, I'm guessing you're also going to get a selection of folks who will flock to the space where the famed Wyatt Flynn spent his last supper," she said. "Not that they are the type of folks who you necessarily want there," she added.

"Hey, I'll take any paying customer!" Colin smiled.

Anxious to move the conversation away from Troughton's Trough, and still preoccupied with the murder from the night before, Hannah cleared her throat. "Hey, did you both hear that Nina – Wyatt's assistant – was taken in for questioning last night?"

Anita's ears perked. "Oh, really? That *is* interesting. I was feeling anxious about another murderer being on the loose in Blairstown; it's nice to hear that they may be close to finding the culprit."

Hannah nodded. "It's nice to know they are moving things along, but I have to be honest. I don't think Nina is guilty."

"Why is that?" Colin asked, briefly looking up from his phone.

"Well, as always, my gut feeling. But the other thing is that I've seen enough murderers in recent days and I just didn't get the sense that Nina could take his life. Or anyone's life, for that matter."

"Knowing you, darling, you already have someone else in mind," Colin said with a kind smile.

Hannah held his gaze and her annoyance edged out a little bit. She should be happy for the success of her boyfriend, of course. He was entitled to be excited about all of the recent positivity surrounding his restaurant. She decided right then to cut him a break.

"It just so happens, Colin, that you know me well. I *do* have another suspect in mind. Liesel Richter confronted me the morning of the murder. I was walking with Mazie, and she ran out of the kitchen of her restaurant to talk to me, with a knife, it was all very heightened."

"That's right," Colin said. "I've been so caught up in preparations for the tasting and the big dinner that your interaction with her sort of slipped my mind."

"Anita, she let me know that Wyatt had written a bad review for *Gutes Essen* and she wanted to warn Colin, through me, with the hope that we'd cancel his dinner. She wanted to protect us. However, she also seemed very, very angry. She had obviously not been able to let go of the review he wrote of her place."

"For good reason," Colin added. "It totally messed with her livelihood."

Anita lifted her brows in obvious interest.

"And I suppose you are waiting for the connection? Well, it just so happens that Flynn's body was found near Liesel's restaurant." She dropped the information with pride.

"Sounds like a good lead to me," Anita agreed.

"I do think that the combination of the location and the motive; Liesel wanting revenge on Wyatt, it all adds up.

I think it's time to confront the woman, especially so we can save poor Nina from the false charges."

"This sounds promising," Colin said. "I know I usually join you on these trips, but unfortunately, I'm slammed with all of this new restaurant stuff. That said, I'm worried that you are inviting trouble if you confront Liesel alone – especially if she really is guilty."

Hannah waved him away. "Not at all. Remember, this is what I do for a living. I can more than handle my own," she argued.

Colin placed his phone face down on the table. Concern etched on his face. "Honey, I'm not trying to tell you how to do your job, but I really am worried for your safety. Would you consider taking Kate and Mazie along for backup?"

Hannah's face turned up in an instinctive smile at the mention of her precious beagle. And having Kate Carver along for the ride wasn't at all unappealing. She liked the plan. "You know, I think you might be on to something." She smiled at Colin.

He nodded, satisfied. "Good, that makes me feel much better."

Hannah called Kate and told her of the plan. Kate agreed to meet her at Jolt of Java without hesitation. She would happily be Hannah's wing-woman as she confronted the jilted owner of the German restaurant. Of course, it would also benefit her own investigation if she went along with Hannah.

Spurred by the hope of finding the killer, Hannah finally felt like she could finish her coffee. She gulped down the lukewarm latte and felt the buzz of caffeine jolt her to action. "I'm ready," she said.

Anita and Colin waited with Hannah until Kate arrived at the coffee shop. "I walked here," she said. "I didn't want to come in my patrol car in case it spooked Liesel."

"Oh, good thinking!" Hannah exclaimed. "The good news is that *Gutes Essen* isn't at all far, so why don't we all just walk there?"

Mazie had been happily snoozing on her bed by the fireplace in the store, but at the mention of the word walk, she sprang to life. Hannah chuckled. "Looks like we're all ready to go."

It was still early enough in the morning that most restaurants weren't yet open to the public. Hannah looked at

Kate as she put her hand on the front door to Liesel's store. "Wish me luck!"

"Good luck," Kate whispered as she followed behind Hannah. The door was unlocked. The two women stood in the threshold of the empty dining area and glanced around the room. Hannah wasn't sure what she was looking for exactly, but she knew enough to keep her eyes open at all times.

"Hello?" Hannah called through the empty room. "Liesel? Are you here?"

The women heard dishes clinking from the kitchen. Hannah gestured for Kate to join her as they approached the room. "Hello?" she called again, this time a little bit louder.

The dish noises stopped at once. "Who's there?" Liesel called.

"It's me, Hannah Barry! I'm with Kate Carver." Mazie stood between them, wagging her tail. "Oh, and Mazie!" Hannah added.

Liesel emerged through the swinging door to the kitchen, wiping her hands on her apron. "Oh, hello, ladies. What brings you here today?"

Kate jumped right in. "Good morning, Liesel. I'm sure you've heard the terrible news."

Liesel stared at Kate expressionless.

"About Wyatt Flynn?" Kate prompted.

Liesel gave a knowing nod. "Indeed, I have."

"Any thoughts about the tragedy?"

Liesel released a disgusted grunt. "Thoughts? Oh, I have plenty of those. I guess the main one being, that I was not upset to hear the news. I know I'm probably not supposed to say that. We should never celebrate death, of course, but there is no love lost between us, I'll tell you that much."

Hannah listened carefully. Generally speaking, a murderer wouldn't be quite so open about her motives with the chief of police. It made her second-guess her opinion about Liesel's potential involvement.

Kate continued her standard line of questioning, asking about her whereabouts during the time of Wyatt's death, why she disliked him so much, when the last time she saw him was, etc. Meanwhile, Mazie's nose was working overtime, sniffing every square inch of the place. Hannah took the opportunity to follow Mazie around to see if she'd come up with anything Hannah might miss. They traveled the perimeter of the room, then moved into the kitchen. Liesel was so engrossed in her conversation with Kate, she didn't even notice them slide in behind her.

As soon as they stood in the kitchen, Mazie started growling. Hannah looked down at her dog in surprise. Mazie hardly ever made that noise. She was much more of a sniffing, tail-wagging type of dog. She dropped her leash to let her investigate whatever was making her so upset.

The dog scampered over to the trash bin and dug her nose in it, sniffing and pulling things out with her teeth. Hannah watched the mess she was making and glanced back toward Liesel and Kate. She would clean it up before anyone had the chance to be dismayed at the mess. She watched as her dog tore through virtually every scrap and wrapper in the bin, until her growling stopped, along with her whole body.

Hannah moved toward the dog to see what she'd found when Mazie popped her head out of the garbage can and turned to Hannah. Gripped between her teeth, Mazie had locked onto the handle of a knife. The same knife Liesel had been carrying when they'd run into her on their morning walk. Hannah took a careful step toward her dog, not wanting her to make any sudden movements. Upon closer look at the blade, she could see that it had dried blood on it. *A knife in the garbage?* Hannah thought. *That is odd.*

Hannah spotted a piece of fresh bread on the counter that it smelled like had just been taken from the oven. Hannah ripped off a small piece and held it in front of Mazie. Sure enough, Mazie dropped the knife and trotted towards Hannah in favor of the treat. Hannah quickly picked up the handle of the knife with a paper towel, deciding to clean up Mazie's mess later. This seemed more urgent. She went back through the swinging door and approached the two ladies.

"Kate," she interrupted, brandishing the large knife. "Mazie found something."

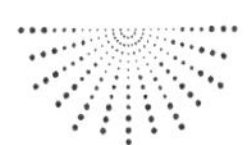

CHAPTER EIGHT

*L*iesel stared at the knife, looking confused. Then her eyes traveled to Hannah. Hannah stood wordless, and Liesel looked back to the knife. "What is that?" she finally asked.

"Um, it's a knife," Hannah said, unable to disguise her disdain for the woman. Playing stupid wouldn't get her out of a murder charge.

"Right, I know that. I mean, where was that? I haven't seen that thing in forever. I certainly haven't used it for a while."

Gotcha, Hannah thought. "May I remind you that Mazie and I both saw you holding this knife a few short days ago. When we saw you on the walk, you were holding it." She leveled her stare at Liesel, daring her to lie about it again.

Liesel's eyes went wide. "I, um. That one, I don't think that's the same..." she sputtered.

Kate reached into her purse, and like any good detective, revealed a plastic bag marked "evidence". "I'll be taking that piece of evidence," she said, reaching for the knife.

Liesel, who had finally seemed to find her words burst out, "It's only dried blood from meat! I promise you. I work in a kitchen, at a German restaurant. We deal with animal blood every day! I promise you, that is not Wyatt Flynn's blood. I had absolutely nothing to do with his murder!"

Liesel's eyes were wide, and she seemed panicked. *I would be too if I had just been caught red-handed with a murder weapon,* Hannah thought.

"Should we take her in?" Hannah asked Kate.

Kate shook her head. "No, I was able to ask her all I needed to just now in terms of questioning her, but..." she turned to look at Liesel. "Don't' even think about leaving town. We are going to test this knife to see if you are telling the truth. If you aren't guilty, you have nothing to worry about," she said, her voice flat and professional.

Hannah watched Liesel's response. She did seem to calm down slightly, wiping her sweaty palms on her apron. "Okay, good," she muttered to herself.

Hannah wasn't convinced, of course. *She's probably just an amazing performer.* She pulled Mazie closer to her, wanting to put distance between her dog and a potential killer.

"We'll be in touch very soon," Kate said and the three of them left the restaurant. Hannah was careful never to turn her back to the restaurateur.

Outside *Gutes Essen*, Kate turned to Hannah. "I'm going to head to the station and get this tested right away. The sooner we know if she's a real suspect, the safer the whole town will be," she said.

"Okay, thanks so much for coming with me today. Colin was right, that would have been a little scarier if I had been alone!"

The women hugged goodbye, and Hannah turned in the direction of Troughton's Trough. She wanted to tell Colin all about what he'd just missed.

Hannah arrived at Colin's restaurant to see a line snaking around the block from the front door. She couldn't believe it; the place hadn't even opened for the day! She turned and headed to the back entrance to avoid the crowds. When she slipped into Troughton's Trough, she saw Colin surveying the crowd from inside. "Can you believe it?" he said to one of his managers. "I would never have imagined that a little tasting of ribs could ever have resulted in this. It's incredible!"

The manager agreed.

"But we obviously need to order more supplies. I hadn't considered this when I ordered ingredients for this week. Could you go see if you can double everything from the supplier? I know it's late notice, but we have to ask," he said.

The employee shuffled to the back room.

"Hey," Hannah called, sensing an opening to say hello.

He turned to see her and brightened. "Hannah! Look at this! Can you believe what you're seeing?" he asked her.

Hannah shook her head. "It's pretty incredible," she agreed.

He showed her his phone. "Check this out. Clair's vlog has even more views, but the best part is that they are actually translating to customers. People from out of state have even been calling to see if we can do a delivery across state lines! I mean, this is insane. I could open up a whole new arm of the store, I could turn this into an empire!"

Hannah loved how excited Colin was, and felt grateful to share this big moment with him. But she had to admit that something about the whole thing felt odd. Could it be that his success happened at the same time that a food critic who'd had his last meal here had been murdered? One had nothing to do with the other, of course, but it gave her a sinking feeling. She smiled at Colin.

He turned to her, beaming from ear to ear, and stopped short. "What's wrong? Why are you fake smiling?"

Hannah groaned inwardly. Why did he have to know her so well! "Colin, I'm so happy for you. I want you to hear that loud and clear."

He stayed listening, knowing she wasn't finished.

"It's just that somehow it feels a little bit morbid to take pleasure in profiting off of Mr. Flynn's death." She cringed at how her words had sounded out loud.

"Profiting off of his death?" Colin asked, incredulous. "Clair's vlog had nothing to do with Flynn dying. That man was frumpy and mean. No one liked him, and his murderer could have been any one of the restaurant owners whose livelihood he seared with his nasty review column. I got lucky he died when he did, it saved me from the same fate!"

Hannah gasped at his statement.

Colin stopped short. "No, I didn't mean it like that. I was just trying to say that I have not been profiting from his death. Directly. Not at all. The vlog is why people are coming here. The death was an unfortunate incident that sadly happened near the same time." Colin looked worried now, as if he was afraid he'd crossed some kind of line.

Hannah was silent as she processed what he had just said. Then, though she knew she shouldn't say what came to her mind next, she couldn't help herself. "Colin, where did you go when I left the restaurant that night?"

He looked confused.

"After you were finished washing dishes. Did anyone see you go home?"

Colin narrowed his gaze on her, causing a chill to run down her spine. "What are you asking me, exactly, Hannah?"

She cleared her throat. "I'm just wondering where you were when Flynn was murdered."

"You have got to be kidding," Colin said, anger creeping into his voice. "Are you actually accusing me of slipping off into the night to end Flynn's life?" His eyes were wide, and he was frozen to the spot.

Hannah quickly shook her head no, that hadn't come out right.

"Not only is that absurd, but it's also offensive. It means you don't really know me. It means you think that I'm capable of something like that. How could you date someone who you think could ever commit murder? Hannah, what are you saying?" His voice had lost its anger now and was pained.

"No, no, I'm sorry, Colin. That came out all wrong. What I am saying, though, is that I think you should distance yourself from Clair's vlog."

Colin scoffed. "Right. You want me to distance myself from the very thing that is bringing me all of this business? Dare I ask your reasoning?"

"I just think that basking in Clair's vlog is akin to dancing on Flynn's grave."

Colin threw his hands in the air. "Are you tired, Hannah? Have you not slept in a while? What's going on with you? No one is dancing on anyone's grave! She gave me an amazing review. I'm doing what any normal person would do and capitalizing off of it. It has nothing to do with Flynn."

Hannah's voice went soft. She knew she couldn't explain herself properly at this moment. "I just want to remind you that only a short while ago, you said that *my* approval was enough."

"Hannah, you and I celebrate each other's accomplishments. We support one another. Of course, your approval means the most to me, but I'd be crazy not to take advantage of this free publicity. It's basic business. Nothing personal," he said. He moved toward Hannah with his arms outstretched as if to give her a hug when his phone rang. He stopped midstride to take it.

"Hello? Why, yes, it is! Thank you, that's so kind! Let me get to the books and I can see what we can work out," he said, moving to the reservation tablet. He winked at Hannah and pointed to the phone, then gave her a thumbs up.

Yeah, I am happy for you, Hannah thought to herself, wishing she believed it. She and Mazie turned to the door to leave when she saw the line of people standing there. She redirected herself to leave through the back entrance with her beloved beagle, and a heavy heart.

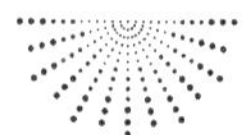

CHAPTER NINE

After taking Mazie for a little stroll in an attempt to lift her own spirits, Hannah found herself at the police station. She wanted to talk to Kate about the two current suspects.

Kate had just been finishing up a sandwich at her desk when Hannah came knocking. "Hannah, come in. Do you have anything new for me?" she asked between bites.

Hannah took a seat across from her friend. "I don't have anything new for you. In fact, it might be just the opposite," she said.

Kate stopped chewing and waited for more.

"I've been thinking about both Nina and Liesel. I'm

having trouble calling either one of them a murderer. I wanted to hear your opinion," she said. She was doubting her own opinion, thanks to her recent exchange with Colin. She was afraid that her own feelings were getting in the way of her reasoning abilities. As evidenced by the way she all but demanded her beloved boyfriend give her an alibi for a murder!

"Right, then." Kate wiped her hands and slid a pile of papers in front of her. "Nina has shared more about Flynn's abusive treatment with us, but she also keeps defending him. This could be a sign of how dysfunctional their relationship really was, or it could point to the fact that she really did have an appreciation for him, which would make her less likely to be the murderer."

Hannah nodded along. "That's the feeling I got, that she did enjoy working with him, and maybe more, that he didn't treat her very well, but not necessarily that she would want to kill him off," Hannah agreed.

"Which brings us to Liesel." Kate moved another pile of papers in front of her. "The results from Liesel's knife came back."

"Wow," Hannah said, impressed with the speed.

"I know, I had them expedited. It turns out that there is no sign of Flynn's blood on the knife. Anywhere. It's one hundred percent animal blood, just as Liesel said it was." She clasped her fingers together and placed them on her papers. "Which is to say that I think you may be right about neither one of these women being our prime suspect. Unfortunately, I don't have any other leads. Do you?"

Hannah leaned back in her chair, and Mazie jumped up on her lap. She stroked the beagle's soft, furry ears as she thought through the question. "I'm hesitant to mention this one because I can't tell if my feelings are driving my suspicions or if she's actually suspicious," Hannah confessed.

Kate's eyebrows raised. "Why don't' you tell me your suspect, and I'll use my neutral perspective to help figure that out."

Hannah nodded. "Okay, I like that idea. So, Clair, the vlogger, well, she is back in town," Hannah began.

"This is the one whose viral video has put Troughton's Trough on the map, correct?" Kate asked while taking notes.

"She's the one," Hannah confirmed. "It seems she has spotted another opportunity to keep herself relevant, by way of Colin's restaurant. I heard through the grapevine that she is planning an entire video series based around every item of food that was part of Wyatt Flynn's last supper," Hannah said.

Kate placed her pen down and leaned toward Hannah. "Wait, what?" she said, dropping her detective guard. "As I recall, this is the same person who stood up in the restaurant and all but yelled at Flynn, correct? It's not as if the two of them were buddies."

"That's absolutely correct," Hannah said. "They were rivals in the industry, old guard vs. the new. She's a little more relevant, edgy, has more followers. But to exploit his death like that, even if it was a friend of yours, it just feels a little off to me," Hannah said.

"Hmm. In my neutral opinion, I think your feelings are not wrong about this one," Kate said.

Hannah breathed a sigh of relief. "Oh, good. I'm so glad to hear that. I'm just so worried that Colin is going to go along with her scheme," she added.

"Why would he do that?"

"I know he feels a certain debt to her for making his restaurant so famous. And doing a thorough evaluation of each of his meals wouldn't necessarily be bad for business, it might not attract the typical customer he usually has, but I think I heard him say recently that customers are customers."

"Yikes," Kate said. "I can imagine wanting to capitalize off of recent publicity, but I sure hope he wouldn't go along with this last supper thing Clair has planned. It's in poor taste."

"Exactly," Hannah agreed. "However, things between us are somewhat strained right now, and I'm afraid I can't be the one to tell him that. I'm not sure he would listen to me after I interrogated him about his whereabouts the night Flynn died."

Kate swiveled her head towards Hannah. "You did not."

"I know – see?! I'm losing my touch!"

"Ha, Hannah. You aren't losing your touch; you are just jealous. Of Clair or of his success, I'm not sure, you're going to have to work that out, but your P.I. instincts are still intact. Don't second guess yourself."

"Thanks, Kate. I needed to hear that. I really do love Colin, and I hate the strain between us right now."

"What are you going to do?"

Hannah placed Mazie back on the ground and scooted her chair back. "I'm going to find a way to get through to him."

"All right, good luck to you. I'll keep working away over here. Let me know what you find out," she said.

"I will do!" Hannah said as she left the office. She knew just where she needed to go. Hannah and Mazie made their way back to Troughton's Trough. Hannah would apologize and listen to Colin talk. She wanted to hear all about his business growth, and she wanted him to feel supported by her. Maybe then, when things were back on track between them, she could casually, and nonconfrontationally, bring up her concerns about the last supper project.

She and Mazie walked casually through the sunny streets of Blairstown. The leafy trees were billowing out over the sidewalks. Then they arrived at Colin's restaurant. The crowds were gone, and the doors were locked, which Hanna found strange. It was the downtime between lunch and dinner, but usually, the front door was open. She moved around to the back entrance again and let herself in, hoping to catch Colin in the kitchen.

Instead, she looked up and down the hallway. Just barely in her view, were Clair and Colin. He was sitting on a chair and her head was just inches from his. Her heart caught in her chest. What had she just walked into? She crouched down to cuddle Mazie for comfort when her eyes focused even more, and she saw something strange. Colin's hands were bound to the chair he was sitting in. She hadn't walked into a romantic tryst; she had walked into a potential crime scene!

Hannah moved against the wall for a better view and to be discreet. She saw Colin struggle against the ropes on his wrists and then his head whipped back with surprising force. His whole body shuddered as Clair clasped his hair in her fist, drawing herself closer to his fearful face.

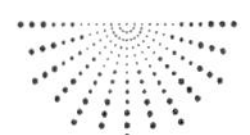

CHAPTER TEN

Hannah swallowed the lump in her throat, feeling like she made a noise so loud Clair would surely hear her. Luckily, she was too focused on torturing Colin to hear anything at all. Hannah quietly slipped her phone out of her back pocket and shot Kate a text message.

Come to Troughton' Trough. SOS. Colin is in trouble. I was more right about Clair than I realized!

Hannah closed her eyes and hoped against hope that Kate would see the message and get there quickly. She stayed crouched against the wall, watching as Clair gripped Colin's hair tighter. His head jerked against the force of her grasp. Then she saw the movement of feet just out of her view. Someone else was there. The shiny dress shoes of a man made a clicking noise across the floor, and Hannah caught a glimpse of who it was; Jordan, Clair's assistant.

This was good information to have as she sat there, trying to decide how to help save her boyfriend. Right now, it was two adults against one adult and a dog. Mazie was a former police dog, which gave her a leg up, but Hannah still wasn't confident the two of them could storm in there without finding themselves in deep trouble. She had to be smart about this.

"You need to remember that it was my vlog that brought you notoriety in the first place. You are not showing the appropriate gratitude," Clair's voice shot out like poison.

Despite his fear, Colin had not lost his nerve. "I never asked for your support. And now that I know about you, I would NEVER want the support of a killer!" he said.

Hannah stifled a gasp. Though she could have surmised as much given the scene before her, it was still a surprise to hear the words come out of Colin's mouth. Clair really was the killer?

"You would never be able to prove such a thing," she replied.

At this, Colin let out a wicked laugh that surprised Hannah. "That's what you think."

Clair leaned in close enough to Colin that Hannah was sure he could feel her breath on his cheek.

"When you came back to town, I had a feeling something fishy was going on," he said. "So, I went to your hotel room at the Briar Motel."

Hannah leaned her head toward them so she could hear more. He'd done what? Why hadn't he told her? When had he found the time?

"That much we know, Sherlock. You're lucky we didn't kill you right there where we found you instead of dragging you back here to your restaurant."

Hannah gulped.

Colin continued, "I searched your room and found a knife."

Clair released the back of his head by shoving it violently forward. "What are you talking about?" she said it as a demand more than an ask.

"Something didn't add up. You hated Flynn too much to want to do an entire series on him, even if it brought you the views and analytics. I wanted to see for myself if there was something else going on."

Clair circled his chair, arms crossed as she listened.

"The knife was from my table settings. I sourced them myself from Argentina, so I'd know them anywhere. And it was covered in dried blood."

Hannah's whole body tensed at his latest revelation.

"Great detective work, we commend you on your abilities, don't we, Jordan?"

Clair's assistant had been standing, arms crossed, watching the exchange. Hannah wondered what his job was, exactly.

Clair stopped in front of Colin's chair. "Too bad you didn't get the chance to exit the room before we arrived, isn't it?"

Colin said nothing.

"My story about Flynn's last supper could have worked wonders for me and for you. It's your loss that you chose to sabotage yourself and your business. Really, I mean what kind of businessman are you?" Her voice was sardonic, Hannah had to stop herself from storming in to tackle her right then.

"Now, I'll have to find a new way to exploit the life and death of that revolting Wyatt Flynn. Too bad you can't profit off of it with me." She nodded to Jordan, who took a step towards Colin. "Anyway, I can't leave any loose ends behind. Where did you put that knife from my room?" she asked.

Colin said nothing, but he made the mistake of looking at his legs.

Clair's eyes flashed. "Jordan, search his back pockets."

Jordan moved to hoist Colin to his feet, an awkward move with his hands still bound to the chair, but it was enough to provide him access to the back of Colin's jeans. Sure enough, he'd been sitting on the murder weapon. Hannah watched in horror as Jordan turned the knife over in his hands.

Clair held her hand out for Jordan to pass the blood-crusted knife to her. "I was settled in the knowledge that the poor, abused Nina would be held to blame for Wyatt's death. After all, I couldn't have created a more perfect murderer profile if I had tried. And of course, if she fell through, we always had the bitter old Liesel who hasn't stopped complaining about her negative review since Wyatt left it."

Hannah gritted her teeth at the fact that Clair had tricked her so easily. She had assumed the real killer was either one of those ladies. Now she knew who it really was.

Hannah frantically checked her phone for any sign of Kate having received her message. There was nothing. She was going to have to do something.

Clair moved toward Colin with the tip of the knife aimed at his throat. "Maybe those same suspects will be considered for killing you off as well," she said, lurching for him.

She was only inches from Colin's throat when Hannah charged forward from the dark hallway just as Colin cried out in anticipation of death.

A startled Clair looked in their direction as Mazie flew through the air and clamped her teeth around Clair's slim ankle.

CHAPTER ELEVEN

Clair screamed in pain as she dropped to the ground, releasing the knife on the way. She swatted at Mazie in an attempt to get the dog off of her.

It was then that Hannah grabbed the knife for herself and moved to Colin, quickly slashing his wrists free from the ropes tying him to the chair. Colin rolled his wrists and stood quickly, facing Jordan, the last remaining threat. Jordan actually took a step back and put his hands in the air in surrender. It was enough for Colin, who groaned and fell into Hannah's arms.

"Hannah, thank you for coming! I am so sorry for my behavior lately. I've been distracted and full of myself. There is no excuse for it. Thank you for putting up with me. And for saving me!" he said, burying his face in her arms.

Hannah held Colin close, happy that he was still alive, and that he was saved the fate of Wyatt Flynn. There was no doubt now that Clair had been the killer, and that she wouldn't hesitate to do it again should the need arise. "Of course, I forgive you," she said bringing her head to his.

The two of them stayed embraced for a moment longer before Hannah spoke again. "But why did you go to the Briar Motel without me?" she asked, unable to resist the question, even at that moment.

Colin managed a good-natured laugh. "Well, I know now that it was a mistake. I will be leaving the detective work to the professionals from now on, while I do my duty as the sidekick!" he said. "I spotted the opportunity and figured I had to get in there quickly. I knew you weren't a fan of Clair's in the first place, and I didn't want to start any trouble in case I was wrong."

Hannah nodded. "I can understand that. Instead, you started trouble and you were right!" she said, bringing him in for another big squeeze.

"It was an absolute mistake," he agreed as a blush crept into his cheeks. "But thanks for coming to rescue me now."

"Of course," she replied.

All this time, Clair had been struggling against a surprisingly sturdy Mazie on the ground. The faithful dog had kept her pinned to one spot without a hope of getting up. "Jordan!" she called. "Get over here, Jordan – help me!"

Hannah and Colin both braced as they watched to see Jordan's reaction. They were read to spring to action and tackle him if that's what it required. And if worse came to worst, they were the ones in possession of the knife.

But Jordan didn't move. His feet stayed planted in place as he stared Clair down from across the room. Hannah made a surprised face at Colin, who lifted his brows in return. What was going on between those two?

"I've been putting up with your antics for the better part of the last three years," he said in a stony voice. "Helping you drag Colin to his own restaurant where you intended to kill him is the final straw!" he exclaimed.

Even with a dog clamped to her ankle and rolling in pain, Clair rolled her eyes. "Oh, please. You didn't even make a move to stop me when I was going to kill this loser," she said, darting a glance at Colin.

Hannah felt Colin stiffen in her arms. "Don't let her get under your skin," she said.

"I thought we stopped an intruder, so of course, I helped you get him here. I did not realize that you would try to kill him once we arrived. I thought you were just trying to scare him. And I did not know that he had found a *used* murder weapon in your room!" Jordan said.

"Try telling that to the police, Jordan," Clair said. "You're about to be the third suspect on the list. This will never fall back on me."

Hannah laughed. "Nice try, Clair. You're forgetting that you have two other eyewitnesses on his side. Jordan was obviously in shock when he saw you attempt to murder someone. We're all just lucky things ended as they did. Even you. Prison time is a lot longer for two premeditated murders than one," Hannah said.

Clair fumed, unable to think of a response. She just kept kicking her feet, trying to free herself from Mazie's vice-like grip.

At that moment, Kate and Ralph arrived, their lights flashing and sirens blaring. When they charged into the restaurant and surveyed the scene, Mazie sensed that she could finally let go. She scampered over to Hannah and Colin, jumping in between them for a long, cozy cuddle. Hannah and Colin smiled fondly at one another.

Clair, of course, attempted to seize the split second of freedom, trying to scramble to her feet, but Ralph's imposing grip came down on her shoulder. "You are under arrest..." his deep voice boomed.

Kate, meanwhile, rushed over to Hannah and Colin. "Are you both okay?" she asked, worry clouding her eyes.

"Fine, thankfully," Hannah replied. "Thanks for coming."

Kate looked up and did a double-take when she saw Jordan standing in the shadows. She rushed over to him, spinning him around, instinctively placing him in handcuffs.

"No, Jordan had nothing to do with this!" Colin called.

"What do you mean?" Kate asked, her hands still firmly around his wrists.

"He didn't know Clair killed Wyatt, and he had nothing to do with her attempt at killing me," he said. "He's clean," Colin said loud enough for Clair to hear, hoping she would realize that her last possible chance of freedom had just slipped by.

"Okay," Kate said, uncuffing Jordan. "Sorry about that, sir."

"Hey, no problem. If I'm not going to be falsely arrested today, there's nothing for you to apologize for," he said.

Kate laughed and patted him on the back. They all watched as Ralph dragged Clair to the back of the police cruiser. When the door closed, Hannah and Colin both let out a big sigh of relief they didn't know they were holding. They looked at one another in realization and started laughing.

Never wanting to feel left out, Mazie took the opportunity to jump up between them, and landing in Hannah's arms, she took the opportunity to lick both of their faces.

CHAPTER TWELVE

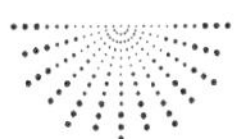

*H*annah and Colin found themselves spending time with one another with a new appreciation in the weeks that followed the incident at Troughton's Trough. Colin felt like he had a new lease on life having looked death so closely in the eyes. While Hannah found herself feeling lucky that she didn't lose Colin. They were both in a bubble of love obvious to anyone around them.

They found themselves at Troughton's Trough one evening after all of the customers had left. Hannah was adamant that they spend as much time there as possible in order to erase the traumatic memory with new, fantastic ones. The two of them sat at the small bistro table on the back patio usually reserved for employee break times. Twinkle lights were hanging in the warm evening air and the sun was dipping below the horizon, leaving a soft, pink hue in its wake.

"Did you see the paper today?" Colin asked her.

Hannah shook her head. "I had a busy day at work, I hardly looked up from my computer. Is there any news?"

Colin smiled and handed it to her. Hannah scanned the front page and released a cry of joy. "No way! Clair has formally been charged with Flynn's murder?" she asked, her eyes looking to Colin. "I wonder why Kate didn't text me," she said reaching for her phone.

When she glanced at the message icon and saw the little red "thirteen" there, she said, "Oh. I guess she probably did. Like I said, I was just so busy!"

Colin chuckled. "I think a few of those might be from me."

Hannah smiled, flipping to the full article on the third page. Colin waited quietly as she read through all the details of the charges against Clair. "She won't be released on bail, that's fantastic," she muttered. When she finished, she placed the paper back down and sighed. "Boy, am I ever glad that matter has finally been dealt with," she said.

"Same here!" Colin agreed. "Along with the many other lessons I've learned along the way, I now know to take any praise I receive with a grain of salt."

"Oh, Colin! Don't let the fact that she's a murderer get you down. Even killers have taste buds," Hannah joked.

Colin rolled his eyes. "I suppose there are still benefits to the critic's favorable review. Folks are still coming in thanks to her vlog."

"And then there is that whole new clientele who's coming in as a result of the murder and the killer both hanging out here!" Hannah said. Indeed, there had been a whole new set of customers who came in curious about Flynn's last meal, as well as Clair's arrest.

"I'm still so thankful that the media didn't find out about the fact that I was held hostage in my own restaurant!" he said. "Not that it's stopped people from coming by, fascinated by all of the sordid events leading to her arrest."

"Well, at least you aren't going to exploit her arrest or Flynn's death," Hannah said. "Right?" she winked at her boyfriend, knowing he never would.

"I mean, on the other hand, I could create a prefix meal for people. Maybe I could call it 'A Meal to Die For'?" he joked.

"No!" Hannah clapped a hand to her forehead. "You wouldn't!"

"Or I could do one called, 'Last Meal Before Prison'," he joked again.

"Colin, stop. I'm dying over here!" Hannah said in an attempt at her own joke.

"Ha! Nice one. I think we should keep workshopping this," Colin said. "On a more serious note, I have yet to receive any critical reviews from anyone who isn't either dead or a murderer."

Hannah lifted her brows at him. "That's you being serious?"

He shrugged.

Realizing he wasn't kidding; Hannah gave Colin's back a reassuring pat. "A good review from a reliable source is bound to come soon enough. You are an amazing chef," she said.

Suddenly, they saw Liesel looking frantic rush by the back alley where they were seated. Hannah stood. "Liesel?" Hannah called.

"Hannah? Where are you?"

"Over here!" Hannah said moving to catch her in the alleyway.

The other restauranteur swiped quickly through her phone, fumbling with it while muttering, "Hold on, just one minute."

Hannah and Colin patiently waited for her to get to what she wanted to show them. Then she finally turned her phone over to Colin and asked him to read it.

Colin held the phone away slightly so his eyes could focus on it. "What am I looking at?"

"Nina and Jordan started their own food vlog!" she announced excitedly. "Their very first entry is about the culinary delights in Blairstown, Vermont. Press play!" she insisted.

Colin clicked the triangle on the screen. He listened to Nina and Jordan banter with one another and discuss their food finds in the little town. At the top of their list were both Liesel's restaurant, and Colin's.

"They love our food!" she said, jumping up and down. "Finally, my restaurant has been vindicated!"

"Wow. And these two together are dynamite. They have such a great rapport. I can see their vlog really taking off," Colin said.

Hannah, who had been watching over his shoulder nodded. "The best part is, they don't seem to be exploiting the murder to make a name for themselves."

Colin nodded. "That's true. And based on how well this first entry did, I'm not sure they are going to have to."

Colin handed Liesel's phone back to her, and she swiped it, stating that she wanted to show him one more thing. "Read this," she said to Colin. Then to Hannah, she said, "It's a private message to me from Nina and Jordan. They said that the least they could do is profile my restaurant after Wyatt Flynn and Clair Darrow caused so much trouble for us."

Hannah watched happily as Liesel couldn't seem to hold her body still, she was so excited. It was about time something went her way, Hannah thought. She was happy for her.

Hannah also noticed that Colin's mood picked up considerably after reading the message. Even Mazie sensed there was cause for celebration as she stood on her hind legs and tried walking around. It gave the impression she was dancing in agreement.

They all laughed and reached down to pat Mazie, one by one.

"Wait right here!" Colin said, racing into the restaurant. Hannah and Liesel stood waiting for him to return, curious about what he was up to.

Soon after, he emerged in the back with a bottle of champagne. "A toast to our good fortune!" he said.

"Ooh, this is lovely," Liesel said, eying the enthusiastic bubbles.

"Allow me," Hannah said grabbing the bottle. "I should be pouring in celebration of the two esteemed chefs standing in my presence!"

Hannah carefully filled each crystal flute with champagne. Then she lifted her glass to the center. "To great reviews, and to your continued success in days to come!" she said.

Liesel and Colin extended their own glasses to meet hers with a gentle clink. Then they sipped to exactly what Hannah said: continued success in days to come.

IF YOU MISSED any of these fabulous fun cozy mysteries grab the first 6 here or read on for a preview of this great value box set.

Hannah looked up at the vibrant colors on the trees lining her street. The cheerful red and rich auburn of the leaves were in direct contrast to her mood. *How can the leaves be so happy when they are about to fall to their death?* She was just one block from her cozy little house where she'd curl up by the fire, drink some cider, and feel sorry for herself. She just had to make it past his house first. It was enough that she lived one block from Peter Royce, her ex-boyfriend. But now she had to pass by his home every single day on her morning walk. She wrapped her scarf up over her nose and tucked her head down into it. Maybe he wouldn't see her.

It was then that she heard the squeal of tires and watched as a little blue sports car took a tight, tidy turn into Peter's driveway. She felt her blood run cold and her feet involuntarily stopped moving. Out of the driver's seat popped a stylish, petite brunette wearing a shade of bright pink lipstick. The foolish man had always preferred brunette's, saying her blonde was a little washed out.

The new woman slipped gracefully up the front steps of the house and there, waiting for her, was Peter. His tall frame filled the doorway, he wrapped the brunette into a tight squeeze and gave her a kiss on the lips. Hannah knew he hadn't been faithful; that's why they'd broken up. But she didn't think she'd have to watch him with his new girlfriend with her very own eyes. She felt acid rise in her throat and hid behind a big oak tree, taking deep breaths in and out. When she heard his front door close, she looked up to the crisp, blue sky.

Oh, you've got a lot of nerve looking bright and beautiful on a day like today. Can't you see that people down here are suffering? If she couldn't yell at Peter, she'd yell at the sky.

Slamming her hand in her pocket she pulled out her phone. Maybe checking on her precious few house listings would distract her. "Ugh, no alerts!" she muttered and toggled over to her bank app to see what her current balance was. More depression and a big gulp. "I guess I'll have to dip into my savings again this month." Pressing her fingers into the tender skin under her eyes she bit down. "I will not cry today. I will not cry today." However, she did need to sell a house. And soon.

When she arrived at her own cozy little place a smile came to her lips. Colorful potted plants lining the front porch and filling her with joy, she felt her shoulders relax. It was time for that cider. But when she walked up the steps to her door, she was startled by a deep voice.

"Hey cuz! Did you forget we were meeting today?"

Hannah jumped as if an armed thug had just accosted her, throwing her hand to her heart to steady the erratic beating. "Ahhh!" she shrieked, momentarily startled out of her self-pity. Then the familiar curly blond hair of her cousin finally registered. "Niles! Oh, I'm so sorry. I did completely space out our meeting today. But it's so nice to see a familiar face." She let herself sink into the empty spot beside him on the porch swing.

Niles' long legs stretched to the railing. His easy grin turned up at the corners of his mouth. "Well, did you at least remember that I was bringing a surprise for you?"

Hannah lifted her brows in anticipation. "My favorite donuts? This is the perfect day for some of those."

Niles shook his head.

"A macchiato? That would also be a lovely treat."

His grin got wider, but he shook his head again.

"Fine, I give up." She crossed her legs under her body and turned to face Niles.

"I know you've been going through a tough time lately. And I really want to help make you feel better about things."

Despite herself, Hannah felt the well of tears forming. Swallowing, she strained her eyes and willed them not to fall.

"I wish I could be here more to help out, but as I can't... I've arranged for a proxy."

Hannah looked into Niles' deep blue eyes, searching for something to help her understand.

He stood up, stretching to his full height, his head ducking his six-foot frame to avoid a hanging plant. "Close your eyes."

Hannah obediently placed her hands over her face. "This better be good."

She heard the shuffle of Niles' feet across the wood beams of her porch move away from her, and then come back. Then she felt the warm, wet slide of something move up her cheek. "What in the world?" she lurched back in her seat, dropping her hands from her face.

OMG, sitting proudly on the porch swing and staring at her with big, brown eyes shining playfully, was a... dog. It looked at Hannah. Waiting.

Hannah released a nervous chuckle and turned to Niles. "Heh, heh. Good one! Is this your way of cheering me up, by joking about getting me a puppy?" She placed her hands on her lap and gave the dog a sideways glance. It was still staring at her.

"Actually," Niles said. "She's not a puppy. She's three years old, and her name is Mazie.

Hannah looked at the tricolored dog with floppy ears and a long tail. "So, is it a bulldog?"

Niles laughed. "Not a dog person, are you? This is a beagle. They are some of the most loyal, lovable, and intelligent dogs you will ever come across. And this little sweetie is also one of the bravest dogs you'll ever know. She was shot in the line of duty and saved someone's life in the process." Niles scratched behind Mazie's ears, causing her tail to flop cheerfully against the cushion.

An unconscious smile began to form on one side of Hannah's mouth. "Cute. Mazie, you're a cutie." Then she looked at Niles. "Well, it worked, she cheered me up. Thanks for the surprise. Should we head inside to warm up?" She lifted herself from the swing.

"Well, that was easier than I thought it would be. So, you'll take her?" Niles asked.

Hannah spun around to face him. "*Take her*? What do you mean, I thought you just brought her by for a visit?"

Niles' face fell slightly, realizing the miscommunication. "Hannah, I brought Mazie here for you as a gift. *She's* the surprise. She needs a loving home since her injury, and you... well," Niles scratched the back of his neck. "I thought maybe you could use some, er, company." His cheeks flushed slightly as he looked at Hannah.

Hannah's blue eyes went so wide she thought they might pop out of her head and she released a tiny squeak. "Gift? You want me to take Mazie... a dog?" She tilted her head and waited for his response.

As if on cue, Mazie jumped off of the porch swing, walked to Hannah's legs, and rubbed her snout against Hannah's legs before sitting proudly beside her.

Hannah felt something inside of her warm. She noted Mazie's wagging tail. *Mazie is more cheerful than the blue sky. She's ridiculously happy after having been shot. It was like Mazie didn't even remember it happened.*

Niles noticed the way Hannah looked at the dog and went in for the kill. "Look, why don't you just take her for a trial period. If things don't work out, you can give the lovely little Mazie back, no questions asked."

Hannah didn't object, so Niles continued. "Two weeks. Call it an experiment. Call it babysitting. Call it a sleep-over! Whatever you want to call it, there's no pressure."

"Okay. Fine. Two weeks." Hannah's eyes met Niles'.

"Yeah! This is going to be great! You won't regret it. Mazie is the best, you two will be an amazing team."

Hannah reached down to pet Mazie.

"I need to get to work. Crime doesn't stop for any dog, right, Mazie?" Niles waved goodbye and headed to his shift as a state police officer. Hannah watched him leave with a mixture of pride; what a great guy her cousin was, and annoyance; what had her great cousin just gotten her into?

Hannah opened the door and Mazie obediently followed her inside. She crouched down and locked eyes with the dog. "A great team, huh? I wonder what sort of trouble you are going to get into?"

Mazie wagged her tail furiously, overjoyed to be with her new owner.

Hannah couldn't help but note Mazie's resilience, and despite herself, she found a smile crossing her own face.

Read the first 6 books.

Dog Detective – The Beagle Mysteries Book 1 to 6

On the Scent of Murder

Hunting Down the Heiress

Retrieving the Clue

Decked to Death

Dragging Down the Culprit

Adding up to Murder

Murder for the Crafty Ladies and the Clever Beagle

The Art of Murder

If you enjoyed this book, Rosie and Agatha would appreciate it if you left a review on Amazon or Goodreads